Good Bi
by C. D. Moulton

A study of a bi-sexual life in the discovery stages.

Contents

About the author

CD Moulton has traveled extensively over much of the world, both in the music business, where he was a rock guitarist, songwriter and arranger and in an import/export business. He has been everything from a bar owner to auto salvage (junkyard) manager, longshoreman to high steel worker, orchid grower to landscaper, tropical fish farmer to commercial fisherman. He started writing books in 1983 and has published more than 250 books as of January 1, 2015. His most popular books to date are about research with orchids, though much of his science fiction and fantasy work has proven popular. He wrote the CD Grimes, PI series and the Det. Nick Storie series, Clint Faraday series and many other works.

He now resides in Gualaca, Chiriqui, Panamá, where he writes books, plays music with friends, does research with orchids and medicinal plants – and pursues his favorite ways to spend his time: beach bum and roaming the mountain jungles doing his botanical research. He has lately become involved in fighting for the rights of the indigenous people, who are among his closest friends, and in fighting the extreme corruption in the courts and police in Panamá.

He offers the free e-book, *Fading Paradise*, that explains what he has been through because of the corruption.

CD is the discoverer of the Chadam Protocol for curing cancer.

Facebook page Ambrosia peruviana for cancer.

Good Bi

Discovery

It wasn't like this was the first time Mikey Harmon had found himself in an impossible situation. As a matter of fact, it seemed to happen with what was called "stunning regularity" lately. He wondered why he never learned any lessons from screwing up.

Oh well. Grin, act like it's exactly what you expected and bluff it out.

"I'm afraid you lost me there?" he said, trying to sound confused. "Maybe I didn't say what I meant to say. I seem to have that habit.

"What I meant to say was that I didn't see anything wrong with it – if it's what both people want – not that it was something that appeals to me. I like women and wouldn't care for anything else.

"Before I'm misunderstood again, this does not extend to children. I think anyone who brings a child into that kind of situation should be stood against a wall and shot, first in the crotch, then a couple of times between there and the head."

"We agree on that point!" Eileen Smithers replied, with a short nod. "I won't argue that you as much as said you could go for a homosexual romp."

"The truth's somewhere between," Mikey agreed. "I could possibly – I don't know. I've never been turned on by a guy, but it might be possible. What I'm saying is that IF some guy turned me on, I don't see anything wrong with a romp, if he wanted it.

"How did we get on this kick, anyhow?"

"I said I think your friend, Norman, is gay. You said he wasn't, but you didn't see anything wrong if he is. Whatever. It sort of went down that tangent from there.

"Anyhow, I've already made plans for Saturday. Maybe another time."

"Sure! I'll look forward to it!" Mikey returned brightly, while thinking, *When hell is frozen over! Damn!*

Eileen smiled a bit tightly, said "See you later," and walked off. Mikey wanted to run his head into the wall, full speed. *When* would he learn to not do that? All it takes is *keep your **BIG** mouth shut, idiot*!

He sighed. If he was going to have a date this weekend, it looked like he would have to ... that's another *when hell freezes over.*

Crap! That bisexuals have double the chance of a date on a given night thing wasn't funny, all of a sudden. It's like bigot jokes. They're only funny when you're not the target.

What was the matter with him? He was no target here! His only homosexual experience was when he was 16 and he was disgusted by it!

Being honest with himself, after the fact, he wasn't, really. He was mostly scared shitless because he let John What's-his-name screw him, because John was a big deal football player for the high school. Actually, he was more or less neutral about it. He'd expected it to hurt, but it didn't, except one short sharp stab of pain.

Stab of pain. Fitting.

What a mood! What a subject! How stupid!

He sighed again and went into the bar a few steps along the sidewalk for a beer. There were only a couple of people there and he didn't know any of them, so maybe he wouldn't blab the wrong thing at the wrong time, here.

He ordered a Michelob and sat at the dark end of the bar to feel sorry for himself. He had only taken a few sips of the beer when a slightly familiar-looking guy, super-jock type, came to ask, "Mike? Mike Harmon?"

"Er, yes?" Mikey answered.

"John Moorehead. We were in high school together."

Crap! Was this bad timing or *what*!? The same guy who screwed him eight years ago shows up in a bar ten minutes after a girl accused him of being gay!

"I have to admit, I didn't expect to ever see you here, after the way you reacted when we had sex, back then. I really wanted you to screw me, too, but I wasn't in any position to admit I was gay, what with the football team and all."

"Here? You're gay?" Mikey answered.

"Well, I think almost everyone in Bloomberg knows the Pink Pansy is a gay bar!" John replied. "You didn't?"

"I just walked in the closest bar I saw when ... something happened," Mikey said. "I know about the Pink

Pansy. I didn't look at the name. It doesn't matter. A bar's a bar.

"I wish I'd known you were gay! I think I would have enjoyed screwing you, but I was just experimenting, back then, and it wasn't anything I liked. From the other end of the stick."

John laughed. "I'm not busy tonight," he said, raising an eyebrow. "Maybe you'd like to make up for it? Solely from the end of the stick you would enjoy?

"I promise you, you'd enjoy it!"

They joked and started buying each other drinks.

But Mikey wasn't about to let it go past a couple of old friends having a few yucks and a few beers – even if John couldn't have been called a friend. They switched to tequila shooters about four beers later.

Mikey opened his eyes and was surprised he didn't have one hell of a hangover.

This was *not* his room!

It came back to him.

Well, he'd screwed John. Three times.

John screwed him once.

Oh, hell!

Had he liked it?

Well, he definitely liked screwing John. He was, so far as he remembered, still kind of neutral about getting screwed.

John had kissed him. He did *not* like that! At *all*!

Weird. Neutral about getting screwed, but very negative about kissing the guy who screwed him.

Okay. A point for Eileen. He had to say he was bi because he knew right then that he'd let other guys screw him, if he could screw them, too. Maybe he didn't like a man screwing him, but he very damned well liked screwing a man! John was right about him enjoying that! It was almost as good as a woman!

Almost? Why did he think it was more than almost?

Because he wasn't going to knock up a man and get into that kind of trap.

God! He was *really* confused, now! He was laying there feeling guilty and, face it!, very good, physically. Satisfied.

John came out of the bathroom, roughing his hair with a towel. Mikey noted that he had kept his body in great shape since high school. He wished he could stick with some kind of program that would give him that hard-muscled yet slender look.

Hard-muscled?

He almost giggled to himself. Silly romance novel suggestibility.

"Shower's free!" John announced. "Need help?"

"Unless you're a licensed therapist, you couldn't do me any good, in that department," he answered, grinning.

"Actually, I am," John returned. "I went into psychology to find out what was wrong with myself after high school."

"Did you? Find out what was wrong?" Mikey asked, getting out of bed and making a wry face at his blah body in the mirror.

"Yep! Nothing! It's the rest of the world that's screwed

up!" John said. "You were fun. I thought you would be good – and you are. Once you get started, you have no lack of stamina!

"Eggs, toast, and coffee?"

"I usually only have a banana and coffee for breakfast," Mikey replied. "Black."

"Coffee or banana?" John fired back and they both laughed.

Mikey took a cool shower and slipped into his clothes. He would have to go home to change before going to work. He had to admit he hadn't felt this good in years. He didn't feel guilty, either, and he'd thought he definitely would. He was relaxed and felt mostly ... natural. Normal.

Was he actually gay and never knew it?

He looked through the door to John, sitting a pot of coffee on the warmer on the table. He hadn't put on anything yet, and Mikey had to admit that he was damned good-looking.

Okay. He was gay, and never knew it.

He was bi. He was still turned on by thinking of women, but he was also turned on by John – and he could quit lying to himself. He had *liked* being screwed!

Had he liked being kissed by a man? Was he lying to himself about that?

He was surprised by it. Certainly.

He didn't know. Maybe it was a shock reaction.

He was damned confused about a lot of things, all of a sudden. Was he now lying to himself about all of it? Had he actually liked being screwed, or was it only that he was going to go too far in the other direction, now, and convince himself that, because he liked sex, he was gay?

Maybe that was it. He liked sex, and would convince himself of anything that would mean he got more sex. Maybe it was sex itself, not the type of sex.

He went into the kitchen, walked up to John, and planted a long, passionate kiss on him.

Yes, he damned well *did* like it! He expected the tongue bit to turn him off, but it had the opposite effect.

"God, you're a horny one!" John exclaimed. "I'm damned glad I haven't dressed yet! It's a real drag getting in and out of your clothes ten times in the morning!"

"I couldn't hold out for ten, but I'm willing to try!" Mikey replied. "To tell the truth, I'm going to be late for work, now. I can't afford to lose my job.

"Thanks, John. You answered a lot of questions I had about myself. I thought I'd feel really guilty this morning, but I just feel really *good*!

"I know this was a romp, and was for fun, but I do want to see ... sleep with ... fuck you again. The thing that surprises me no end is that I want you to fuck the hell out of me, too!"

"I get home at about seven," John answered, looking him square in the eyes. "If you get here first, you saw where I keep the key. You can bring some clothes or whatever. We'll keep going until we either decide we've had enough of each other or until we die of old age, whichever comes first.

"Be sure you want to learn how far you really want to

go, and that you want to know about yourself. It might only be the newness and the call of the exotic, and you'll end up with a deep psychological trauma when you realize that we all spend ninety percent of our lives lying to ourselves, and only fifty percent lying to others."

"I think I can handle it," Mikey answered, seriously. "I think I already did. I think I not only accept what I am, but I can be very much happier than I've ever been before with it."

"You're queer, and know it?" John asked.

"No. I'm bi, and know it."

"Hmm. You've had limited sexual experience with women, and last night was the first real experience with a man," John mused. "When you planted that one on me, you confused hell out of me. I thought you used that as the wall – we all put a wall up that we won't pass – you could use to say it was only experimentation that you should have gotten done back in high school, now you know, it's been great yuks, have a nice life."

"Then go through the rest of my life knowing I was lying about it," Mikey pointed out. "I don't do that, at least! I just now thought of Eileen and am just as turned on by her as by you – and I am *damned* turned on by you. In the world today, I don't have to do the 'either/or' bit. I can do the 'and' bit!"

"Sheesh! A closet sex addict!" John cried.

"I'm out of the closet, now!" Mikey shot back, kissed John solidly again, said, "See you tonight. Take some pep pills, you're going to need them!" downed the cup of coffee there, picked up the banana, waved, and went to change for work.

He thought a lot about things as he walked to his apartment. He had been living two blocks from John for three years and had never seen him. They moved in different circles – then.

Today was the first day in the new life of Michael Kilpatrick Harmon! It was off to a fantastic start!

"Hey, Eileen!" Mikey called, when he was leaving for lunch. She was walking by on her way to the little restaurant many of the local office workers used. There was little chance she could refuse to walk along with him.

"Hello, Mikey," she replied, coolly. "Going to McCall's?"

"Yeah," he replied. "It's no longer 'Mikey' – it's 'Mike,' from now on. I just wanted to tell you what you said yesterday registered and made me wonder what I really want in the socializing area, particularly sexually."

"Oh. I'm sorry about that," she said. "It's none of my business."

"I disagree. It's definitely your business, if we were to sleep together," he countered, getting a shocked look from her. "I've decided to be honest with myself and with anyone else.

"I went to the Pink Pansy (a more shocked look) and met a guy I knew in high school. I spent the night with him, and we had sex. Several times (she really looked shocked now!).

"Look, I've spent my life to now playing silly games,

trying to get into women's pants, and we both know that's what was going on yesterday. The only difference is that today I'm going to start putting the cards right out there. No more games. I'm going to also tell you I liked the hell out of sleeping with John, and am going to be back there tonight. I'm going to see if I like a lot of things I never had the nerve to try before, and I'm going to be honest with myself, if I like it.

"The sex was both ways, and I'll make another resolution where it's concerned. I will never mention a name again, because sex is private. I just want you to know I slept with a man last night, and will again tonight before I ask you if you want to change your mind about Saturday."

"John? Not John Moorehead!" she answered. "I think two thirds of the women in this town want to sleep with him! I'm jealous as hell! We know he's gay, but he will sleep with a woman, every once in awhile.

"You say you're only interested in getting in my pants, you sleep with guys, and you want a date Saturday?"

"Come on!" Mike said, grinning. "No more games. You know damned well you want somebody to sleep with, on most dates. That's the real object, and the rest is lying to yourself and the world about it. I promise things will be different from anything I've ever done before – even though we've never even dated before – because I'm game to try a lot of things I've heard about, but didn't have the guts to see if it was true.

"Last night, I discovered I'm bi, and that I'm a sex addict. I intend to be very careful, but I intend to get off as much as is physically possible!"

She looked undecided, then grinned at him. "You're on, but it has to start out like a date. Dinner and all that, then we can see if you really do want to try things. I've heard of things that very certainly, shall we say, intrigue me. As with you, I've never had the spine to try them. We can both do perverted things that disgust and repel decent people.

"Do you know how good it feels to be able to be honest about it? – I guess you do! That's where it came from!"

"You know something? I'm as scared as the first time! I'm also going to let go and enjoy every bit of it!" Mike replied. "The old cliché! If I don't like it, I don't have to do it a second time!

"Seven too early?"

"Yes," she answered. "Decent girls need time to get ready. Make it seven oh two!"

They relaxed and had a great lunch. Mike wished there was someplace close where they could have made it an even better lunch hour!

"God! I got into that!" Mike cried. John sat up and shook his head at him, then wrapped around him and said. "Did you ever! You trying to *kill* me!?

"I don't think I ever had sex that good before. I really don't.

"You going to tell that Eileen bitch to hike?"

"Nope! I'm going muff diving, I think, and she's promised to try a lot of things she's never done before. You're showing me a lot of things to try.

"My god! You actually had me so hot before we even did anything I literally couldn't think anything but that I was going to die if we didn't finish it, but I also wanted it to take longer!

"John, I'm a little scared. I don't know if I'm addicted to you or if I'm actually falling in love with you!"

"It's new and chemical," John answered. "I'm so in love with you at this moment I can't even think, but it will get back to a sort of very strong affection, soon. Enjoy it. It's infatuation. Understand that, and it's fun. If you let it get to you, you'll be miserable.

"What I feel right now is that, if you screw that Eileen whore, I'll kill both of you. The reality tomorrow will be that I hope you both get off the best she's ever had and the second best you've ever had!

"We've still got most of tonight for me to try to wear you out to the point you can't handle her tomorrow night!"

"Or for me to leave you so exhausted you hope she'll wear me down so you can get some rest!" Mike said. John was so much bigger and stronger, and had him so wrapped he could barely move at all. John laughed and released him, then quickly turned him over and wrapped him from behind.

Well, he'd said he wanted John to fuck the hell out of him. John was certainly willing to try!

He couldn't remember ever feeling so safe. That was a bit shocking, but it was the only way to describe it. With John wrapped around him, holding him in a way he couldn't move or resist, even if he wanted to, he felt safe. He realized he had never felt safe before. It was a good feeling.

John was wrong. He was falling in love. That scared the piss out of him, on one level, but mostly because John had said he wasn't falling in love, that it would pass.

Was he screwed up, or what? He had this amazing epiphany, understood himself like never before, and was all paradoxes in his feelings, all of a sudden.

But he felt good. He had thought it wouldn't be possible to feel better than he had last night, but tonight was even better. Maybe doing things that destroyed his inhibitions opened up new avenues, in itself.

He knew at that moment he could be totally in love with more than one person at a time. That took the fear of loving John away. It was something that could free him, not something that would restrict or enslave him.

John was moving slowly and was intensifying the sensations by refusing to let the climax come. He hoped it would take all night. It was warm and safe there.

Eileen was moaning lightly, and would tremble with every touch. She gasped and started to move, then stopped. The deal was that he was going to find every sensitive spot on her body, and she was going to lay there, motionless, until she simply couldn't anymore.

He found that his tongue was the perfect implement to find those spots. He was just below her breasts, after spending some time there getting her to the moaning point. He placed his tongue over the kidney, which John taught him was one very sensitive spot for many people, and her body suddenly was jerking and she had grabbed a pillow and was screaming into it.

Well, John had gotten him to the point he was sure he was coming, so he had actually pulled it off with her – before any actual direct sexual contact! Wild!

He held her with his face in her stomach for a minute, then continued, but she was to the point where he could get her off in little time. When he actually got to his destination it took all of ten seconds to finish it.

Another amazement for him. For the first time in his life he was more interested in getting a woman off than in getting off himself ...

... which resulted in him getting off a couple of times when she used the process on him. Always before, he needed a few minutes between, but he didn't, this time!

Then they finished with the mutual bit. What he had called a 69 since before he even knew what sex was. They were both so exhausted then that they went almost immediately to sleep in that position. In the morning, they held each other and had sex in the old-fashioned way. Mike had never known that to be so satisfying, either.

They showered and got ready to go to work. Eileen said she was going to use him for a sex toy, and they were going to try anything and everything they heard about together.

"I think we'll be the best friends that ever lived, but it will be friends who experiment with sex, not some lover thing," she said. "We're being honest, so I'll say that I'll never again find anyone who can come even close to you, with sex.

"I'm a little worried, though. When I find who I want to be the father of my kids, I don't want it to get in the way."

"I think I know myself well enough now that I can promise you it won't," Mike replied, simply.

Experiments

"Larry, you've been looking at me strangely all morning, what's up?" Mike asked of Larry Fields, at the office.

"Oh, it's nothing," he answered. "I ... saw you somewhere, and didn't think you were ... I mean, you were with someone I've known for a long time and.... Maybe it's just a coincidence. Someone you knew, and you stopped in for a drink. Forget it."

"The Pink Pansy, with John?" Mike asked, unconcernedly. "We've been spending a few nights together, lately. It begs the question, if I gave a damn, what you were doing there."

"I'm gay, but I didn't know you are, or I'd have been after you for two years, now."

"I'm bi. I didn't even know that last week, but John and I knew each other in school, and we sort of met accidentally, then ended up in bed. It's a rather ordinary kind of story, I guess. He was attracted to me in school, then I went into that bar because it was closest when a girl dumped me right outside, and he was there. He says nobody loves a rebound situation more than a queen on the make."

"I think anyone would be bi for him. I've been trying to get him into bed for a long time, and he won't tumble. He's very selective, but he can afford to be.

"If you're only bi for him I suppose it would be a waste of time to ask what you're doing tonight?"

"I'm busy tonight, but the afternoon's free," Mike joked. "Strictly pitching, no catching – except with John."

"My apartment's half a block away, so we can go there for lunch, and I'd rather catch than pitch!" Larry said.

Mike was about to say it was a joke, then thought, What the hell? Why not? I'm already getting excited, so last night's wear-down was temporary!

"It's a date," he replied.

"Crazy! That easy! We could have been spending lunch hour together for years!" Larry said.

They went back to their offices. The rest of the day was very satisfying to both of them. Mike learned a little something he was going to try on John.

He was hungry, though. *He* didn't get anything for lunch!

"I fixed some spaghetti from stuff you had around," Mike greeted John. "I was hungry. I didn't have any lunch."

"Oh? Eileen bitch didn't get any lunch, either?" John asked, smirking.

"I have no idea, but Larry, at the office, saw us at the Pansy, and he had me for lunch," Mike answered. "You don't mind, do you? It was only sex. I don't have any special affection for him. He's just someone at the office."

"Larry? He saw us and blackmailed you into it?" John

asked, trying to look innocent.

"No, I saw *him* at the Pansy and blackmailed him into it!" Mike fired back. John laughed, kissed him, and said he was going to shower before supper. They could go to bed early, then get up and go somewhere for a little while.

"Damn! I try to hand you an excuse, and you blow it!" John cried. "So long as you didn't blow Larry, I'll let it pass, but you have to learn to grab an excuse anytime you can."

They teased and played. Mike was almost surprised at how easy and natural things were between them. He was also a bit surprised at how easy it was to be so open and honest with Larry.

Next day, Larry introduced him to Buddy Green, from accounting (who he already knew for a long time), and said Buddy had been interested in him as long as he had, he lived across the hall, so maybe they could share him as well as each other.

"I have to get lunch," Mike said. "Isn't there a sandwich shop on fifth?

"As I said, I'm a sex addict. I don't want to turn down anything that I feel is safe, and I've known both of you for years, so know there's no AIDS or such, and you'd tell me if there's anything else."

"I have stuff in the 'fridge we can warm up," Buddy said.

They agreed to meet at noon at Larry's. Buddy brought over a delicious casserole he'd warmed up, and Mike learned another new thing. It was his first threesome, and, though he'd vowed he was going to pitch and not catch, Larry performed oral sex on him while Buddy screwed him. It was the craziest feeling he ever had when he got off.

He went to Eileen's after work, and they had a great night. He was describing what he had done, and she would tell him about things she'd done. She said a friend had a dildo, so he could see what it was like to use it with her. He said he'd think about it, but not tonight.

The next day he went with Buddy and Larry again, this time with Buddy and Larry changing their position. It was as crazy and as good.

He went home to John after work, and they had a long discussion. He had to agree it was out of hand (and made a joke about that), and that he was becoming a whore, which made something nasty and fatal as much as inevitable.

"I have vacation, starting next week," John said. "Can you get away?"

"I'm due a week and a few days, so yes," Mike answered.

"We'll go to my cabin," John said. "We can spend some time sorting it out. You can't stop the addiction, but you should be able to control it."

"Well, it's really enough, with you and Eileen and Buddy and Larry," Mike protested. "It's safe."

"For now, but what if Eileen sleeps with the wrong one, or Buddy, or Larry, or even me?" John pointed out. "You don't have control of what anyone else does when they're not with you. I'm not going to sleep with anyone else while we're together, but you already are, and that's putting me and Eileen and them at risk. It works both ways. You have to learn to control it.

"See if Eileen can come with us. We have to get to know each other. We can try some threesome things that none of us knows anything about – yet."

Mike asked Eileen, and she could come. They would leave Saturday. Day after tomorrow.

Mike had his one last lunch hour he would share with Buddy and Larry, and told them what was happening.

"We know. You're at the whore phase we went through when we were sixteen or seventeen," Larry said. "We took advantage of you, but you have to admit, you wanted to."

"I still want to, but I have to take control," Mike said. They agreed.

"That's it!" John announced. Eileen said it was as beautiful a spot as she'd ever seen. Mike had to agree.

It was a cliché log cabin set on a knoll by a creek that came from the nearby mountain and meandered on down to a meadow a quarter mile below. They had driven the Jeep for about four miles into the thick pine forest to reach the place.

"Well, we damned well aren't going to be running around on each other here!" Eileen announced. "This would be a place I could spend the rest of my life!"

"You'll be so bored in a week you won't know what to do," John said. "You're the fun and night life type.

"Aren't we lucky? We have a sex addict all to

ourselves, and he can supply what we're both after. We can try to kill him with sex!"

"What a way to go!" Mike cried. "I'm so horny from sitting between you two with the bouncing and such – and with John grabbing the wrong thing when he changed gears!"

"I didn't grab the wrong thing once!" John exclaimed.

They teased and played as they carried the groceries into the cabin and opened it up. John went into the bedroom and came out nude, and said the rule was going to be no clothes. Eileen slipped out of her jump suit and said that was a relief! She wouldn't have to suggest it! Mike left a trail of his clothes as he went for the bed.

They all exhausted themselves – and each other. Mike learned what it was like to be between John and Eileen. It was pretty well up to him to supply the motion.

He did. Getting off was even better than with Buddy and Larry. A bit later Eileen said John was as great as all the women thought he would be.

Then they wrapped up together and slept for awhile. They went to the cool little stream to bathe and relax, then laid on the bank in the sun, close together.

Mike couldn't believe it. He was actually satisfied, and didn't want anymore sex.

For the moment.

"So! How has the week been?" John asked, as they loaded the Jeep.

"I think I learned a lot about myself," Mike answered. "I can control the sex addiction. I'm over the part where

I'll take anyone up on anything. After I wore myself down the first three days, my body adjusted or something. I know sex isn't going anywhere, and it's actually a lot better if I wait until the tension is higher."

"I learned I don't want half the things I wanted when we first got here," Eileen said. "Maybe we all learned something about ourselves. It was really great, John. Thanks."

They enjoyed the trip back to town in almost silence. It gave Mike time to, as John called it, regress.

"Michael! Get your lazy butt in here, right now!" his mom had screamed (it seemed she screamed all the time.) "Your dad will be home any minute, and you know how he is about finding your crap all over the floor! Don't make me come after you or you'll wish you had never been born!"

She always seemed to resent the fact he was even alive. He felt like crawling into a corner or somewhere, but then his dad would really get mad, and he was *not* anyone you wanted to be around when he was mad.

Mike would never forget that day. It was his seventh birthday, and all he got from his mother was a new notebook for school. His father never even said "Happy birthday" to him, or anything, but he never did.

He wouldn't have to worry about never being born because he already wished he had never been born. He would run away, like he did once, but there was no place to go, and they didn't even know he had been gone for two days, the way they acted.

Silas and his girlfriend, Judy, friends of his mother, came over and mom asked if they would watch him, because she and his father had to go to something about his job or something. They would usually just go and warn him to be in bed when they got back, but they always seemed to act really different when any of the family or friends were around.

He remembered how Silas always felt all over him, and how he would hold him and say he was the best kid he knew, and the smartest. It felt really good for someone to say something nice about him. He had that class at school where the teacher said no one should ever touch people in those places, and to tell your parents if they did, but he wouldn't tell his parents anything, because they would say he was a liar and a troublemaker and good for nothing. Silas made him feel good and it felt good to be touched like that.

That night Judy had felt all over him and had licked him and had him feel all over her and lick her boobs and like that, and it was fun, and felt really good. Silas had licked him, too, and wanted him to lick his dong, but he said the teacher had said he was never to do that. Silas said he knew that, and he only said to as a test to be sure he knew about it.

The teacher never said anything at all about the stuff with Judy, so that was alright. She only said if some man did those things, but she was wrong about getting, as the other kids called it, "felt up" by some guy.

Maybe that was because it was that weird guy at the park. The older kids said he would suck all of them off all the time, and he even gave them money, but he wouldn't after they were thirteen or fourteen. He got arrested and that stupid bitch from welfare tried to get him to say he had been felt up and sucked by him, but he never even went to the park, because the older kids kept picking on him and his friends, so it never happened, and she was a stupid bitch he would never tell anything to if he had.

His dad always called his mom a stupid bitch, then smacked him when he even said "bitch" to anyone. Grown-ups were impossible to figure.

Mike remembered how Judy had said he was going to be one sexy stud, and that he was already hung like a stud horse, whatever that meant. She told Silas to knock off the gay shit, because this kid wasn't going to go for it, and he'd end up locked up if he tried it again. That was when Silas told him it was only a test. He said that he had told him to feel him up and jerk him off just to see if he knew, but it felt so good he forgot to tell him to stop and not do it.

Mike told him it was okay, because every guy had a dong and he and his friend, Freddie, felt each other up a lot. They never had that white stuff to squirt all over, though. Silas said that would happen when they were about fourteen, so he asked if that was why the guy in the park wouldn't suck anyone off if they were over thirteen or fourteen, and he said that was probably it, but most queers wouldn't mess with a guy until he did squirt. That was what they wanted.

Silas and Judy showed him what a 69 was then, and

they got all weird and made noises and Judy said they should have Little Mikey around every time they had sex because he turned both of them on so much.

Mom and dad had come home, and Judy and Silas were in the living room on the rug and their clothes were in the bedroom. Everybody yelled at everybody else, and his dad said if Silas didn't give him a hundred bucks he was going to jail, then he told them if they ever came there again it was going to be a hundred bucks a throw. They never did come back.

His mom said they finally found something good about him. Sex. If Silas would pay for him, maybe he could get other perverts to come over and pay for sex with him. Nobody else ever came and paid, but he would have told the teacher about that, because that was somebody like she was talking about that you had to tell on.

Mike was worried about the yelling and jail and stuff, but Silas had paid a whole hundred bucks because he was a real little stud, and he was worth a lot more for sex, but that would end up with the bunch of them in the pen. He waited for Silas to come back for years, but he never did. Dad once said he was in jail in Texas for life, but he never did say why.

Mikey graduated from high school, and was the only one in the place whose parents weren't there. They used the excuse his dad had to go to a business meeting and she was supposed to go with him. Mikey knew they were going to the Blue Moon Bar, because they went there almost every night. He had taken care of himself for more than five years, and was glad they didn't show up because they would have embarrassed hell out of him.

Irene Dimpstone had come to him and said to meet her at Luigi's Pizza, later. He was her personal stud and she didn't want to lose him just because they were out of high school. He'd been going steady with her for a couple of months. He had two girls he screwed before her, but they more or less laid there, and she really got into it. They did a few things, but didn't get into anything kinky. She said he was so sexy she didn't mind risking that her parents would kill her if they found out she wasn't a virgin. He was damned well worth it!

Two weeks later his parents got drunk and a truck ran them off the Partners' Bridge. They had been in the east lane going west. It was two one-way separated lanes, and their little Toyota was no match for an 18 wheeler. Somehow, Mikey wasn't sorry they were dead. Truth be told, he was damned relieved to be rid of them. He got back at them for never having gone to one thing in his life by not going to their funeral. The only ones (he was told) at their funeral were three people from the Blue Moon Bar, and they were there to try to collect money they had lent his mom and dad. They came to the house to ask him for the money, and he told them anyone who lent money to alcoholics for booze deserved to lose it, and get the fuck out of his face.

He sold the house and got an apartment near his job. Irene moved to California, and he had a few on-again/

off-again short relationships before the past several weeks.

"I know why the sex addiction," Mike announced, as they came into the town. "I had sort of hidden the molestation thing and learned that having me there for sex was my only value anyone ever told me about until my last year in high school, and even that was because of sex."

"You were molested? When?" John asked.

"I was seven and this Silas guy paid my parents a hundred bucks," Mike answered. "That was the first time mom or dad ever said I was worth anything. For sex."

"Jesus Christ! Your parents sold you for sex at seven?!" Judy cried.

"In effect, yes. They would have called the police on Silas and Judy if they didn't give them a hundred bucks, and mom said they could make a lot selling me to perverts at a hundred bucks a pop, but no one else ever came," Mike replied.

"You amaze me no end!" John said. "You're so matter-of-fact and casual about it!"

"I think I killed myself, emotionally, when I was about five," Mike said. "It was that or a situation I couldn't cope with.

"John, I love you, and I love you, Eileen. You gave me back some of my ability to feel, emotionally. I've been terrified that I would never be able to actually feel love, and that's where most of the sex came from. I couldn't feel emotionally, so I substituted feeling physically.

"You know something? I don't regret one minute of it!

"I'm not gay. I don't even know if I'm anything specific, and the gay stuff doesn't appeal to me, while I do love being fucked. Go figure. I'm damned glad of everything I've done, and I want to sleep with you – including everything, John. It's not for sex anymore. It's because I love you."

"Mike...," John began.

"No, I know I'm not in love with you," Mike said, simply. "I love you. I love Eileen, and I'm not in love with her. I don't want to let go of the sex. I want to do even more, but only with the two of you until I find the one for me.

"That's my next huge fear. I don't have the least idea of how to be a father, but I want to be a father so I can raise a son and daughter with more love than anyone ever knew before. You can't begin to know how hollow you are if your parents never, so far as you can remember, held you. I have to try to fill that hollow with holding my own kids."

"Anybody else, I'd say you're peeing up a rope," John said. "It won't surprise me for a blink if you pull it off. You are one strong individual."

They went inside, Eileen went home, and they talked all night and most of the next day, then they went to bed, where Mike was made to feel warm and safe. This time, it was physically warm and safe, and emotionally, as well. The sex was comfortable and pleasant.

Mike realized he had substituted one word for sex for

sex with classification labels.

Now he had to learn to separate sex and love. He was fully aware he hadn't begun that process yet. He did know he never wanted to have sexual relations with another man, but he did with John. Lots more, and with new things added. He wanted to *know* what everything felt like on every level.

Was he healing or more screwed up than ever?

Healing

"Well? How was your vacation?" Buddy greeted when he got to the office Monday morning. "Learn anything new?"

"Well, we went to a sort of retreat for the Church of the Living Sun," Mike replied, seriously. "I saw rather quickly that I was lost and adrift, and have renounced sex altogether, unless or until I find my fated bond-mate, and then only to have children to raise in the light of the Living Lifebringer.

"Buddy, I want you and Larry to understand that I was not connected, and didn't know the evil I wrought against you. I wish to make amends. You may flog me with the ritual cat o' nine tails until you feel you have exacted the retribution due me. I beg that you do not take my life, though I know you have that right. I have done you terrible evil to so use and abuse you."

Buddy looked as though he would faint on the spot, his mouth hanging open in disbelief. Mike broke out laughing, and said, "I wish I had a picture of the look on your face!

"Buddy, lover, it was a fascinating and fabulous foray into the inner psyche, and I'm through with the sex addiction, I think. I had a great time with you and Larry, and enjoyed every second of it, but I'm through with sex with men – except John. I doubt I'll ever really let go of the fagot part, altogether, because, despite everything else, it was truly a wonderful experience, and it seems kind of natural, in a weird sort of way. Maybe I don't have to tell you how safe and warm I feel with John wrapped around me. It doesn't even seem paradoxical to feel safe while some guy is fucking me, and that's still a little confusing, but it's the way it is, so I'll accept it.

"I suppose I'll still experiment a lot with Eileen. We have a really good thing going, and I don't mind mentioning her name to you, because you talk to her all the time, and she knows about you, and she said she tells you all kinds of things she wouldn't even tell her best girlfriend. She says you discuss me – in excruciating detail."

"*And* John!" he agreed. "She really got into him, and he even said he would marry her to have kids, but she has to understand that he's queer, and that will *not* change! She said she actually might! She could wait to fall in love and end up a basket case because she has a tendency to pick the abuser type, which John would never be."

"They could be content together, which is one hell of a lot more lasting than happy," Mike agreed. "They could also share me!"

Buddy and he both laughed, but the look in Buddy's eyes said it was probably no joke. It wouldn't surprise him for a minute if they actually did get married – and shared Mike.

Was Mike through with the sex addiction?

He himself had decided to settle down with just one fifty times, then someone would always come by and he turned right back into a whore. It was pretty well under control, with just a few safe people like Larry and Bill, but he knew damned well a certain type of guy could raise an eyebrow and he'd get on his knees so fast it would make your head swim. He was probably fated for something pretty horrible, as a result.

He very sincerely hoped that would never happen to Mike. Mike was a special person. He would cry when he couldn't have him again, for awhile.

Mike heard his name called as he returned to the office at lunchtime, and turned to see two people he'd met for a moment at the Pink Pansy coming toward him. He waited, and they suggested he spend the afternoon at their place. He said he wasn't going with anyone but John, and that was that. One of them started about "John, and Buddy, and Larry...." and he answered that he was selective, even when he would go with almost anyone who asked, and that they wouldn't be included, even if he hadn't passed the whore phase. One of them made a snide remark and slapped him. He came back with a blow that knocked the jerk against the wall, where he slid down to slump onto the sidewalk.

"Care to try for two?" Mike asked the other one, who put his hands up and looked like he would turn tail and run, any second.

Mike strolled away with the one trying to revive the other.

That actually felt good! Why did he picture his father's face when he smacked that asshole?

Cripes! Another neurotic phase starting? Was he going to start striking out at people, picturing them as his father while he beat them to a pulp? He wouldn't need John's expertise to explain that one!

Don't get extreme. He hadn't beat anyone to a pulp, he'd struck back at someone who hit him first. That was all. He had never hit back at his father (he would have been beaten to death if he had, and knew it) and this was a psychological reaction to violence against himself. He had controlled it. When he saw his father's face he was tempted to keep beating the jerk.

Okay, he was neurotic, at least, and knew it. Control was the answer.

Two women from the office were waiting by the door, and each gave him the eye while they tried to get him away, so he said to just say whatever. They put on an innocent act and said they just happened to be there, and didn't mean anything except to welcome him back to work.

Bonnie Gooden, the blond one, went on into her department and Martha Nikols, the brunette, walked with him, and said it was a lie, and he obviously knew it, and they were both *very* interested in him, because the skinny was that he was a bona fide sex addict, would do anything, and they wanted get him alone to see if it was true. If so, she was free tonight.

He didn't need this! He really would like to take the afternoon off with the two of them to try a threesome with two women and him.

"I am a sex addict, and I would do anything, but I have to stop it before I do a lot of damage to myself and everyone I care about," he replied. "I would like nothing better than to get both of you in bed tonight, but it mustn't happen."

"Why not? What would it hurt?" she countered.

"Besides my self-esteem?" he answered. "Well, it could hurt you and her if I've taken a tumble with someone who has something nasty or fatal, couldn't it? That's inevitable if I don't stop it. As you said, as soon as I start, I'll do anything. It's fantastic fun, but also dangerous as all hell."

She sighed. "You go with guys, too?"

"Well, I'm as much as living with John, and I've done all kinds of things with a couple of other guys," he replied. "There truly were no limits. I have no control, once I start, so I won't start."

She sighed again, and said, "I suppose I'll get to work and spend the afternoon thinking about you. If you backslide, I'm right in there." She pointed to the shipping department.

He grinned at her, she went into dispatch, and he went to his desk, where Larry caught his eye and looked moon-eyed at him. They both laughed.

"Well?" John asked. "I think you made it through one day without sex!"

"Ah, but the day's not over, I said only with you and Eileen, she's not going to be here tonight, and I'm horny as all hell!" Mike fired back. "To tell the truth, it isn't so bad after I get into the job. It's a matter of not thinking about it. I did start thinking about you about half an hour before quitting time, and got hornier and hornier.

"Shall we shower before dinner?"

"Among other things," John answered.

Half an hour later they were exceptionally clean and very satisfied. John fixed a chicken and asparagus casserole that was truly delicious, then they went out for a couple of beers and to talk with people. The word was out that hitting on Mike could get you smacked in the puss, so everyone made it plain it was just joking – though it really wasn't.

"John?" Mike asked, as they were walking back to the apartment.

"Yo?"

"I don't get it," he said. "I don't see myself as sexy. I'm sort of turned off by myself when I look in a mirror.

"I mean, I'm not flabby or overly soft, even though I'm tighter now than when we met. I'm ordinary-looking. From what little I've seen, I'm on the larger end of size, but not to any great extent.

"I mean ... what's the big draw?"

John thought for a minute, then said, "You're honest and you're uninhibited. You have a slender build that makes you able to move in a lot of ways ... and your eyes are fantastic. They say, 'Want a quickie?' to everyone you meet.

"I really don't know. You just are. Maybe you're

spraying pheromones around, or something, but I've noticed that most people, male and female, give you speculative looks all the time. I don't think they even realize that's what they're doing. You're so used to it you don't notice. It doesn't happen unless you're there in person. I doubt anyone would react to a picture.

"Remember Don Williams?"

"The guy in school who was so good-looking you wanted to smash his face in?" Mike asked. "I never could figure that. He was mostly a nice guy, but he seemed to grind people the wrong way, for some reason.

"I see. He had the looks, but there's just something about him that repulses people."

"He's a big star on the soaps," John explained. "Women see him on TV and flock to the stage door, convinced they're in love. They'll hang around for hours, just to get a glimpse of him, and stay that way until they get within a few feet. You can see the attraction disappear in seconds.

"I was at a taping, and by the door, when a couple of them were a few feet away when he came out. He didn't say a word, just smiled and went on, and they walked away saying he was a total jerk, and they couldn't figure what they ever saw in him.

"Mike, he didn't do one thing! He smiled and walked by. He didn't say a word.

"It's a weird world we live in, sometimes.

"I was studying him and the phenomenon, and got to be sort of a friend. We hit the sack with him strictly, as you say, as the pitcher, and he was exceptionally good with sex, but he had almost no experience. We talked about it a lot. We tried various types of deodorants and such, in case it was the pheromones, but nothing seemed to work.

"He married Irene Gregorson. The super model. She was the same, so far as being beautiful, nice – and repulsive, and they got along together quite well. They have two kids that people like, so there's a chance it's not the kind of thing you inherit. The kids will be awfully goodlooking.

"Ask me, they're aliens!" He grinned.

"Well, alien," Mike agreed. "I've had time to get horny."

It was a very pleasant night for both of them.

"Hi, sexy!" Larry greeted. "Boss wants to see you."

"Thanks," Mike replied. "Any idea why?"

"Probably wants to bed you," he answered. "She had a bunch of papers, but I don't know if that's what it's about."

Mike nodded, and went to tell Quita, the secretary, that he had word the boss wanted to see him. He was passed right into the office, where Violet Vernors, the section head, was sitting with Harold Franks, the office gossip/toady.

"Please have a seat, Mr. Harmon," she said, sternly.

Uh-oh! She always called him by his first name! Franks was looking smug.

"What seems to be the problem?" Mike asked.

"Problem?" she asked.

"I've gotten past playing silly word games with people," Mike explained. "I'll be totally honest with you, you be honest with me. I'm not here for nothing, and you're very formal, so something's wrong."

"Very well," she replied. "Why are you frequenting gay bars and living with a known homosexual?"

"None of your goddamned business!" Mike snapped back. "Next question? Don't let it be a personal one that has nothing to do with this place, you, or my job.

"What's that got to do with you?"

"We have reports that you're frequenting gay bars and living with a known homosexual, and that reflects on this place," she answered. "That makes it my business."

"Well, you might ask yourself why the person or persons who make those reports would know about it – unless they also frequent gay bars," Mike said, sourly. "I hope you've gotten signed and notarized statements from my accuser, because you're damned well going to need them. They won't help you, but it will allow me to include them in the suit."

"Suit?" she asked, looking nervously at Franks, who was suddenly not nearly so smug.

"Even mentioning sexual orientation in this situation is sexual harassment," Mike explained, like he was talking with a retarded three-year-old. "Your only defense is to present your source, which will allow me to sue the piss out of him, her, or them, as well as you. Might as well make it a collective case.

"Care to continue this session?"

"Let's not let this get out of hand!" she cried. "I have

to investigate anything that may reflect badly on this company! It's part of my job!"

"Investigate what?" Mike demanded. "In what way has my private life, which I've gone to great extremes to keep private, reflected on this company? Who, except someone who was there, would even know about it?

"Don't get me wrong. I'm not defending anything I've done, or anyone I've done it with. It doesn't need defending, because it's simply none of your or this company's business.

"Again. Ask yourself, under those circumstances, how your informant even knows about it.

"Anything else?"

"My only recourse is to terminate your employment here," she replied.

"Because of gossip about something in my private life that this company or you have no legal status to even mention?" Mike said, smirking at Franks, who was sweating, now. "How droll! That should be good for a couple mil more from you and your informant!

"I can consider myself fired?"

"I, er, have filed it," she mumbled.

"Okay. I'll clean out my desk and go. I suppose I'll stop by the Pink Pansy for a drink," Mike said, happily. "I'll even buy Harriet, here, a drink – just to show how magnanimous I can be."

"It's not because of that!" Franks cried. "You got into a brawl right outside of the door of the place!"

"I never got in a brawl outside of any door," Mike snarled. "A fagot from the bar slapped me, and I decked him. I don't know how you ... oh. You're his sugar daddy, aren't you?

"He's going to turn into the most expensive trade you ever turned, I guarantee!

"Got to run. I'm cooking supper tonight, so I can use the day to make up a really great recipe! Eileen ... how come you didn't mention that I sleep with her, too? ... is coming over.

"Catch you later! In court!"

He walked out with the two of them staring wide-eyed at him.

He really was as furious as he could ever remember being, but was used to controlling such things, so they didn't show.

He thought a minute, then called John, who suggested he actually get a lawyer and sue the bunch of them. It was a case they couldn't defend, so he couldn't lose. He said he'd also see Franks shunned by any other queen in the state, because you just didn't do that.

"I don't think he's actually gay, he's just a disgusting office gossip," Mike said.

"He's damned gay. You nailed him about the trade bit," John corrected. "He's also, if what I've seen and heard, a bit too fond of underage boys. He's the type who gives the rest of us queers a bad name."

They talked for a few minutes, then Mike called Eileen, who knew a bunch of lawyers. He told her about it, and she said she would get him an appointment with a really good lawyer, within the hour.

"I can't afford any lawyer," Mike pointed out.

"Ha! This is a lawyer's dream! A real 'can't lose' case," she replied, laughing. "You'll even be able to bid the price down with them!"

She got on another line, then told him to go to Patterson, Masters, Williams and Goldstein at two – and to make it plain that he'll go elsewhere if they won't give him a break.

"See Ed Bloom there. He's good and fair," she finished.

"Ed Bloom, at Patterson, Masters, Williams and Goldstein?" he asked.

"It's a weird world," she shot back.

"You get no argument from me on that!" he agreed. "Coming over for supper and an all-night threesome?"

"Uh-huh!"

"Well! At least, on this one, you won't have to go through the embarrassment of a public trial with everything you ever did in life spread out for the world to see!" Ed Bloom said, happily. "If there ever was a case designed to be settled out of court, this is it!

"We usually get thirty percent, but you've got your deal. I'll have Barbs – that's Miss Morton, if you're listening – prepare the contract at twenty, and we absorb half the costs. If I'd gotten this one out of college I'd be retired and living on a Caribbean Island since I was twenty two!

"I'm really surprised. I met one other person like you in my college days. I'm not gay, even a little bit, but there was something really sexy about him. He wasn't a movie idol type or any of that, but people had a sexual response to him. If you give me the secret we can make it ten percent!"

"Not free?" Mike asked, grinning. He liked Ed, who seemed a lot more honest and ethical than any other lawyer he'd ever met.

"FREE?! I'm a *lawyer*!" Ed cried, looking shocked. "What? You don't watch us on TV? Sue your doctor! Sue your best friend! Sue your mother! Sue Social Security!" He laughed.

"You want to smack them in the puss," Mike agreed. "Why did you allow the profession to sink to that?"

"Politicians," he replied. "Most politicians are lawyers, and they're that type or they wouldn't be politicians."

They chatted about politicians and lawyers awhile, then Ed said he'd be in touch with the first settlement offer in a day or so, probably.

"How much should I sue for?" Mike asked.

"Start at fifty mil and settle for ten," Ed counseled. "More, and you end up in court and on TV."

"I don't mind," Mike answered. "If you want to go for half a bil and settle for a hundred mil, I'll go for it. You can charge me fifty percent for that!"

"No. You won't come across well on TV," Ed said, seriously. "What you have is something that only works within ten or fifteen feet. On TV, you would end up with a couple thou to tide you over until you get another job. Let's keep it within the bounds of possibility. With this, the company will want to avoid publicity. That's the only thing you really have."

"You're the counsel," Mike said. "Actually, I would have left that company in a couple of months, as soon as I lined up something else. It's a dead-end nothing job, really. I don't care to sit at the same desk for the rest of my life. I was sort of surprised that Vi would do anything like that, but want to see Franks' face rubbed in the shit he's causing. He's a really disgusting worm."

"Want to spend a little of the money you'll make on spec going after his ass?" Ed asked. "Let's see how pure his life is, where he can say anything about anyone else?"

Mike looked thoughtful. "Go for it! That one, we can demand a lot of publicity on! Let the office gossip learn what it's like from the other end!"

"Isn't that what the case is about?" Ed asked, seriously, then grinned. Mike laughed, gave him the finger, then said, "I kind of like it from either end."

"Or in either end," Ed countered. They laughed again, then Mike went to the grocery store to get stuff for dinner.

"Well! It seems you're going to be a millionaire!" Eileen said, putting the wine on the table. "Ed says this one is a true dream of a case. He says he really likes you, because you don't make a big phony facade for people to see. You're pretty much what you seem to be.

"John is in some kind of situation where a guy is holding off the police. Hostages and all that kind of thing. It will be on NC, so we can turn it on and watch."

"Stand-off? Is it dangerous?" Mike asked. "John isn't

in any danger, is he?"

"A little, but he's done this before. The cops call him when they need a psychological expert."

Mike flipped on the TV and found the news, where the scene was dozens of police cars, ambulances, news trucks, and a lot of people just milling around. The announcer was saying, "... since just after four o'clock this afternoon. It seems the family is being held in a room in the center of the house, so sharp-shooters from S.W.A.T. can't get a shot. The wife is reported to be injured, but we have no way to know how seriously. Dr. Moorehead is in contact with Mr. Sommers by tele-phone, and is trying to determine the exact extent of the ... something's happening. Joe?"

"Yes, Paul. Dr. Moorehead has talked Sommers into allowing the wife to come out for medical attention, but is holding her mother and his own two children. Dr. Moorehead is trying to convince him that it would be smarter to let the children go as well, because they don't even know what's going on. It would be a ... here she comes. She doesn't seem to be harmed, and is carrying the wireless phone, which puzzles me, because she ... what the holy hell!?"

A woman had come out of the house and had brought a pistol from her pocket, which she was using to fire at random into the crowd. A S.W.A.T. man stood and shot her four times before she could get another shot off. She dropped.

"Joe? She shot awfully close to you, by the looks of it. Are you alright?"

"I'm hit. I don't think it's too bad. A medic is right here, so I will ...."

"Joe? Joe? Are you alright? Joe? JOE! ANSWER ME!"

The remote camera focused on a man laying on the street with two medics working over him. One of them picked up the microphone laying there and said, "Back up! Give us air! Get the ambulance here, stat!" He was speaking into the microphone and a walky-talky at the same time. You could hear the faint reply that the ambulance was on the way. What is the condition of the patient?

"Critical. I think we can hold on if we get attention fast."

"Ten four. I'm almost there. If I have to run down a few of these idiots I damned well will! What is the *matter* with people!"

The camera suddenly went to the front of the house, where John was going in the door. A S.W.A.T. man was running toward him.

"Dr. Moorehead is entering the house. We lost focus on him in the confusion ... Gil, take over please."

Another voice came on. "This has turned into something that is totally unexpected and strange. It appears the wife, Lily Sommers, was using the phone, disguising her voice while pretending to be her husband. The condition of the others, those we assumed were being held hostage, is unknown at this time. Dr. Moorehead is taking a chance I wouldn't have the balls – sorry – intestinal fortitude to take. The situation is out of control, and not even definable at this time. He may be walking into a trap, but he has shown extreme courage in tense situations before.

"We have a link to the walky-talky the S.W.A.T. man is carrying. Let's listen.

"... trying to get him to use more caution, but he says the people in here might well be injured or in danger. I mean, she was nuts! There's no telling what she's done! We're ... the door's open to the ... OH, DEAR GOD! Jesus H. Christ! Oh, dear god!" There was a definite sob in his voice. "I can't take this! Oh, god! They're all dead! Those little kids! They're cut to pieces! Oh, god! I've never seen anything like this! Get the fuck in here! Oh, god!"

The entire S.W.A.T. team and a number of police were running for the door. There was total confusion. A cameraman with a hand-held was running for the door, then was trying to push inside, then the scene was from his camera just as a policeman reached for the camera. The scene tumbled, then went blank. The only words were the cop, saying, "... cut up in there and we need doctors, not some asshole bastard son of a bitch motherfucking shithead reporter!" The sound went out, too.

"Er, it seems that cameraman was a bit, er, overly, er, excited and ... we have an update from the medics. Our field man, Joe Longstreet, is in critical condition, but is expected to make a full recovery. He is being rushed to Mercy Hospital, where an immediate operation will be performed.

"We will monitor the situation here carefully, and will not make further comment until we have something to ... there comes Dr. Moorehead now. Maybe we can ask him what is happening inside."

"I really, *really* wouldn't *do* that!" Eileen warned.

"Dr. Moorehead! May I have a quick word?" a reporter yelled, running toward John.

"There are dead people inside. We don't have time, and I don't have nearly the patience to put up with tabloid reporters," John warned. "I intend to see that felony charges are brought against anyone who has or does interfere with police and/or doctors. Clear enough for you?"

"Yes. Is it true that, as reported to me, the little kids were cut up and tortured for hours, burned with cigarettes, and sexually mutilated before they died?"

John stared at him for about five seconds, then decked him. He looked at the camera, which was a bit shaky by then, said, "Back to you, Jim!" and walked away.

"*I told* you not to do that!" Eileen said. "Mike, John's going to be awfully torn up about this."

"I reckon!" Mike replied.

"What I'll never get over is the way those tabloids stretch something as horrible as that into something much worse," John said. "It was the worst thing I've ever seen. I did all the wrong things, but I have the consolation that the deaths of those children came before I was even involved."

"How in *bloody hell* can you say you did all the wrong

things?!" Eileen demanded. "What else could you do?"

"I thought I was talking to the husband," he explained. "I was saying to give the wife the benefit of the doubt, because those highly charged emotional situations were almost never what they seemed, at first. He – or she – said it was definitely true, everything, and that she had actually slept with half the men in the neighborhood, and she was pregnant by one of them.

"I said that was not necessarily so, that there was an even chance he was the father. After all, he did have two children with her.

"She argued that one was his and one probably wasn't, and he had a vasectomy, so this one couldn't be his. She deserved to die. She had gone too far to ever go back.

"I should have seen the clue then. She said he was always a straight and true husband, and had given her the benefit of the doubt a hundred times, even when there really wasn't any doubt, and she rewarded him by sleeping with a few more bums she met on the street. It was because she had married him when she was pregnant with the first one, and was too scared not to.

"Cripes! That should have told me something was dead wrong there, but I was so tied up in being the hero that it went right over my head!"

"For Christ's sake! It was done before you even got there! You said so yourself!" Mike cried. "You can't blame yourself for any of that!"

"I could have prevented her from going out there and shooting three people so she could commit suicide by cop!" he replied. "I'm just glad they weren't all as serious as that reporter. At least he'll recover, and there won't be that to carry around."

"It saved the taxpayers a few million dollars they would have had to spend trying her and keeping her housed and fed for the next seventy or eighty years," Eileen pointed out. "She was determined to go out that way, and did. You couldn't have made any difference in that. I'm a woman, and I know how she was thinking. She killed her own children, and she would never be able to live with that. If you'd gotten there before that, you could have changed things. You didn't. You didn't know anything about it. You're probably responsible for saving a few lives because you put her in check when you showed up. You made her see it was hopeless, and all she could do was make it worse. I don't think she meant to hurt anyone seriously, she just wanted them to shoot her so it would be *over*!"

They talked for several hours. Eileen answered the phone for awhile, then unplugged it. They came to the door, then, and Mike said the next person who knocked on that door was going to the pen for malicious harassment. He called the police, who said they certainly would put a man out there to see no one else bothered them. They damned well *would* charge anyone who tried to get past him with malicious harassment!

They slept with Eileen and Mike holding John between them.

"... Moorehead was, beyond question, the hero of the day. It has been determined that the husband and children were dead for more than an hour before he was called, and police profilers and hostage experts, as well as Capt. Holding of S.W.A.T., inform NewsPoint that the simple fact Dr. Moorehead kept her on the phone, talking, prevented her from becoming a sniper who might have killed a number of innocent people. We here at news center have now determined that she was a certified sharpshooter. Mike Harmon, a close friend of Dr. Moorehead, says he and others had already determined that the distraught woman went out that door, pulled the pistol from her wrap, and fired into the crowd in a way that was meant to only slightly injure one or two people, but would ensure that the police and S.W.A.T. team would kill her. It is called 'suicide by cop' by the national media.

"We are assured that Joe, our injured reporter, will recover fully, and will suffer no permanent damage. He jokingly says that at least now he can swap tales with the big boys.

"There will, of course, be a thorough investigation of the actions of everyone involved, and the charges of impeding a police officer will be brought against two reporters from out-of-state tabloids. One of them is in hospital at this time with a broken jaw, the cause of which was witnessed by all the people who watched this tragedy unfold on NewsPoint. Police Sgt. Mike O'Reilly says he will also be charged with assault against a citizen acting in an official capacity for the city. Forty thousand people watched, right here, as he charged at and struck Dr. Moorehead in the mouth with a microphone. We of the legitimate press deplore all such tactics, and will supply video-tapes for the police as well as to Dr, Moorehead, should he choose to bring civil suit against that reporter, Frederick James Ganyon of The Angry Voice tabloid.

"In other news, the traffic accident that took two lives on the inter...."

Eileen turned the TV off, and said, "He charged you and struck you in the mouth with a microphone?"

"It did look that way from the angle behind him," Mike agreed.

"Well, he shoved the mike in my face, and it did hit me, but it had that foam pad on it," John replied. "Why did you two hand them that shit about suicide by cop?"

"Because it's true, and you know it," Mike answered. "You probably did stop the crazy bitch from killing somebody else."

"Whatever, you can sue that tabloid, Mike can sue Violet and Franks, and we can all live disgustingly comfortably cruising the Mediterranean in your private yacht for the next fifty or so years," Eileen said. "Meanwhile, I have to get to work. See you tonight. I'll have to tell all about it at least five hundred times, I suppose."

She put the back of her hand on her forehead and threw her head back in the old silent movie exasperation move, sighed heavily, winked, and went out.

"What's for today?" John asked.

"We could go back to bed for awhile," Mike suggested.

"I really need that right now," John agreed.

<u>*Reality*</u>

"Want to settle fast and silent with the company?" Ed Bloom asked. "You get two point five, and the company admits to nothing."

"Does it include Franks?" Mike asked.

"They want it to, but they'll leave him out there twisting in the wind in a blink," Ed replied. "We can get him for a couple thou or so is all, so that's not a big deal."

"Okay, settle with the company, but we make it nasty for that little gossip," Mike agreed. "I don't care if we don't get a penny from him, but I want the next one of his type to stop a minute to think before they try that kind of thing."

"I know a court reporter who's a homophobe, so he'll be happy to destroy that one with a short article, then we drop it because we never meant for it to get into the tabloid mentality type of case?" Ed said, smirking.

"Done! What do I do?" Mike answered.

"Sign here that you'll accept the company offer, but that there is an exception about any other parties. They are not included in the settlement agreement."

"Go for it. Right here?" he signed, and a secretary witnessed.

"Okay. Tomorrow morning's paper will carry an interesting short, and we'll meet here at about ten to be embarrassed at how far it went and to decry the excesses of the tabloid press," Ed said. "I'll have Barney here. He knows what I plan. He might be a little mean because you're bi, so ignore it, okay?

"You decide how you're going to word it so it sounds more or less spontaneous and natural."

Mike nodded, then went home to tell John they were millionaires.

"'... Franks, who is a known homosexual around town and is considered to be a mean-spirited gossip, even among his peer group. The charges he then caused to be brought against Mr. Harmon had nothing to do with his job – which Mr. Harmon felt it better to leave than to cause the firm embarrassment, true or not – but the company was embroiled in the affair, regardless of their policy of not interfering with the personal lives of their employees unless and until such things became a matter of bad reflection on the company. The company, which we will not name as they are not involved in this part of the matter through any fault of their own, felt they had a duty to pay Mr. Harmon enough to support him until he finds other employment, has stated they have and will give Mr. Harmon the highest ratings for his resumé. His work is exceptional, and he will always be welcomed back, though they are aware his reputation has been stained, and that it would prove difficult for him to interact with other employees.

"Attorney Edward Bloom stated to this reporter that the

case was entered merely to ensure that Franks' penchant for spreading unfounded and negative gossip against his fellow employees should make anyone associated with him cautious of allowing him access to information about their private lives. 'Franks is a petty, mean, little snake who will sneak up behind you and bite you on the ass at the least opportunity, so beware!' Bloom stated. 'This kind of thing disgusts decency, and has to be stopped!'

"The suit is for one dollar, and is, as stated...." Mike read. "Well! I think I'll have to chastise my lawyer severely for allowing this to go beyond the company group, don't you?"

Eileen and John laughed. "Well, be home early enough for us to go shopping for a yacht and private jet!" Eileen suggested.

"Either one is more than a lousy two mil," John pointed out. "We can maybe get a sixteen-footer and a used Piper Cub.

"Seriously, Mike, what are you going to do with the money?"

"I think I'd like to travel a bit," Mike answered. "Let's go to some of the places we'd all like. We can spend a year getting rid of the money, then come back here or to someplace we all like and get jobs and live like we were normal. We've fooled them this long, so we should be able to pull that off!"

They joked and played awhile, then John and Eileen went to work while Mike went to Ed's office to be surprised that the very tabloid-mentality hack reporter who printed that embarrassing article in the morning's paper was there. Mike waved at the secretary and barged into the office, then looked apologetic, saying he should have stopped out in the waiting room, but was so upset he stomped right past the receptionist. He'd wait until Ed could talk with him.

"You should be here for this," Ed said. "Mike Harmon, Barney Jeffers and Gordon Killian."

Mike "visibly stiffened" and made a very short nod toward Jeffers and Killian.

"Mr. Killian is Mr. Jeffers' editor," Ed explained.

"I see," Mike replied, shortly. "I came here because of that story in this morning's paper to give you a little – a *lot*, really – of hell for mouthing off.

"Ed, what ... how could you do that?"

"It was off the record, I thought," Ed answered, innocently. "I damned well won't ever say a *word* in front of Barney again! About anything! I thought we were friends!"

Killian was looking at Ed, and Barney winked at Mike, who winked back.

"Damn it, Ed! If you'd said it was off the record more plainly I would never have printed that bit!" Barney defended. "You said it was the result of a petty fucking little shithead of a worm spreading stories, and, off the record, you thought he should be drawn and quartered! I thought that was the only part that was off the record!"

Ed aped being shocked, himself (Come on! A bit overdone, Mike thought) and said he might have done that.

"Now, let's not let this get blown out of proportion," Killian pleaded. "It's a misunderstanding, and it will definitely make it known to anyone who associates with that little fagot exactly what he is. Those queers are all alike."

"Let's not sit in a lawyer's office in a conversation you know is being taped and make statements that can be construed as hate-motivated," Ed snapped.

"Not to mention that I'm bi and am living with another known homosexual," Mike agreed.

"Er, I understood you were living with a woman, an Eileen Something," Killian said, looking shocked.

"I am. Bi," Mike replied. "I can say from experience that the old joke about having double the chance for a lay on any given night is true! The only difference is that sometimes I'm the one getting laid.

"Look, let's really don't let this get blown up too big. You have a point in that now everyone will know to avoid that little turd, so I'll drop the case if you'll print that your story may have been slightly exaggerated. and that I didn't mean for it to go so far – although, on reflection, I did.

"We can all forget it and get back to our lives. I just want to go somewhere for awhile until this dies down. People are the same as they always were, and it's getting ridiculous. How about we shake and agree to start over. Next time Ed can make it very plain when something's off the record, and – Barney, was it? – can be a bit more careful about what he prints.

"Deal?"

"It works for me!" Barney agreed.

Killian looked relieved, and said that was very kind of him, and thanks. Ed grudgingly agreed. They talked a little longer and Mike made sort of friends with Barney, while Killian stayed stiff and a bit haughty. Barney and Killian left, and Ed had Mike sign some papers, then said he was due in court. Mike went to the little café in the lobby of the building for coffee and a pecan Danish, and Barney came to sit across from him.

"I'm interested in some things, and this is definitely not on the record in any way," Barney said. "It's sort of personal. *Very* personal."

Mike nodded and said he saw that this would happen in Ed's office, that it was why he came to the café – that served really putrid coffee.

"It's just that I don't pretend to understand the gay or bi lifestyle, and you seem more than willing to discuss it," Barney said. "I mean, you seem like a more or less regular sort of guy, and Moorehead makes no secret of the fact he's que ... gay.

"I really don't know what I want to ask. Moorehead's a jock who could have been big time in the NFL. He's handsome enough that even I wonder what it would be like to sleep with him. He does sleep with women, and they rave about him being some kind of superstud.

"I'm confused, I guess. It really sort of scares me that I would even consider sleeping with a man. From pictures, I couldn't see what anyone saw in you, to tell the truth, particularly anyone like him. In person, you're really the kind of guy who could be your best friend, and there is some kind of ... sexual tension around you.

"Could you find a question in that and answer it? I'm kind of homophobic, and know it, so I'll understand if you tell me to fuck off."

"Well, John is a psychologist who studied a lot of genetic science in his degree," Mike replied. "He says there's absolutely no doubt whatever that homosexuality is what he calls a mixed dominance genetic factor, which is why a given person can be as totally hetero as Killian, as very slightly bi as you, as totally bi as me, as strongly homo as John, or as totally homo as Franks. Macho, bi, fagot. It's genetic, but it's basically the religious influence that prevents a flat statement by science.

"It's kind of funny, in a way. I really like to fuck. Anybody. I'm a sex addict. I had to learn to control it or I'd end up with something very nasty and horrible, like AIDS. I've done that control bit fairly well, now.

"I was really surprised to learn that I like being fucked. John and a couple of others can make me feel really good while they fuck me.

"As to the oral thing, I don't really like that – from the sucker end – at all, except a sixty nine, and that only with John. I guess I love him more than I've ever loved anyone before, and even that's not 'in love' in a real sense. I love Eileen the same way.

"I know why. I'm genetically bi, but I mean the sex addict part. Trite as it is, it's my mother's fault. She was willing to sell me to any pervert who would give her a hundred bucks for me when I was seven, believe it or not.

"Anyhow, that's over and done and unalterable. You can't unring a bell. I'm very comfortable with my sexuality, now. I wouldn't give up any part of it. I *like* to fuck and I *like* being fucked."

"I might be able to let some guy like Moorehead fuck me, and I suppose I'd like fucking a guy as much ... well, not nearly as much ... as a woman. I had one blow job when I was about fifteen, and was so scared I don't know if I liked it or not. I was sure I was going straight to hell if I did, so I kind of blocked it out. The guy who blew me was too big to fight, so I've felt guilty since because I didn't fight him anyhow," Barney said. "I suppose that's what's really behind a lot of homophobia. I've heard that most homophobes are latent que ... homosexuals who are afraid they are, which is why they're homophobes."

"I don't mind 'queer' or even 'fagot'," Mike said. "Labels don't bother me. I never used those words, except when talking with the guys or something, and never did consider them to be very negative ... well, 'screaming fagot' is always negative, and even most of us queers use the term in a negative sense.

"You have to be Catholic."

"I'm the typical Catholic," Barney agreed. "I'm a Catholic, but not a *good* Catholic. The mea culpa guilt trip bit is drummed into me, so I react that way. It's the only thing I really have against Catholicism. No matter what, you're guilty of something, and that screws you up in just the way we're talking about.

"You say you love Moorehead, but aren't in love with him. Could you be in love with a man?"

"Yes, I think so," Mike answered. "Please call him John. The 'Moorehead' bit is almost a put-down, and I'll be defensive as all hell, where he's concerned."

"Sorry," Barney answered. "Reporter mentality. You speak of the subject in an impersonal form. Use the sir name.

"I guess I really envy you. I'm jealous that you can have a date every night. I wish I was as ... uninhibited as you."

"You have to resolve your own self-image. You have to find out once and for all if you're actually queer, and to exactly what extent," Mike counseled. "It's perfectly normal to be gay to one extent or another. The trouble comes when we want everyone else to be the same as we are. It's not real. It ain't gonna happen.

"I know two guys, gay, who would really go for you. You're their type. You're slender and tight, and you're not at all bad-looking. You're clean and take care of your body, and you might be surprised at how important that is to most queers. The clean part, particularly.

"*Not* now, but consider it carefully. Be absolutely certain you want to know yourself that completely, and be as sure you can let your inhibitions go completely. Determine that you are going to do *anything* up to the point you know you simply couldn't, then I'll introduce you to them.

"This will include whether you want to be in the middle of a threesome – which can be about the craziest get-off, and the wildest, you can imagine. You can't imagine it because it's not anything like anything that's ever happened to you before. One will be fucking you and the other sucking, or even doing a sixty nine with you."

"I know I could never suck a man," Barney said. "That can't happen. I think, if I was being sucked, I could let a man fuck me at the same time, but I don't know at this moment if I would like being sucked. I think I would. I think, if I'm honest, I did, but I just knew I was aimed straight for hell if I admitted it."

"Could you kiss a man?" Mike asked.

"I never wanted to, if that's what you mean," he replied. "I don't suppose ... not with the tongue bit, but I'm not too sure about that, if I'm hot enough, at the time. It might be kind of sexy and kinky, especially if I knew I was going to fuck him."

"Or if he was going to be fucking you," Mike said, grinning. "I know how far I'll go if I'm hot enough, and that's almost anything. If you haven't been anywhere close before you don't know.

"I'm sitting here with a hard-on. I'm a sex addict. Talking about sex gets me hot."

"I am, too," Barney confided. "I hope nothing happens that makes me have to stand up suddenly.

"Want to go somewhere and find out how far I might go?

"My god! I just made a homosexual advance on a guy! I don't believe this is happening!"

"You don't know how tempted I am!" Mike said. "I

think I could get you to do a lot of things you'd never considered before, and I think you'd enjoy hell out of it. That's the sex addiction I have to control.

"That girl at the counter would go for a quickie, and then you could think about it when you're not just overheated. You would be awfully easy to take advantage of, right now, and you'd do something you might regret. You have to be certain you can cope with it, or you get more and more screwed up."

Barney thought for a minute, then nodded. He said he'd get his satisfaction with her or another girl he knew, wait a little while, and make a decision. He might call later.

He dropped a five on the table, swung his laptop in front of his crotch, and went toward the girl at the counter. Mike grinned to himself, thought, *I'll give it fifty-fifty. He's probably curious enough to try it and he'll damned well be a player from then on!*

He went home to make a sandwich for lunch.

"Mike? Barney here,"

"Yo, Barney! What's the skinny?" Mike grinned at John, and put it on speaker.

"We were discussing different lifestyles earlier, and I did as you suggested. I went home with Donna Marie, the girl at the restaurant, then came home here to think about what I was doing very carefully," he answered. "I think I can let go of my inhibitions enough to try some of it, but I'm not sure I want to be on the, uh, receiving end of anything yet."

"Then you're not ready," Mike replied. "If you're not

sure, then end up doing some things you told yourself you wouldn't, you'll end up with the same guilt complex you told me about, but reinforced. You really do have to find where you *can't* go and dump the inhibitions totally to that point.

"Believe me, I didn't think I was going to be on the receiving end of anything, either, but it turned into the threesome thing I told you about.

"I didn't have any reservations along religious lines, or any of that stupidity, I just meant to save that end of it for John. As I also said, you do things when you're hot that you'll regret later if you haven't resolved your own thinking on it. It can end up with your upbringing making you feel you're a fagot for doing those things and intelligent consideration won't make a tiny damned bit of difference.

"I don't have any religious upbringing at all, so I can't really say how I'd react if I did. Those old brainwashes can be awfully hard to set aside. John will tell you that some people can't be reprogrammed, it's so embedded.

"Really, Barney. I like you, and I don't want to see you screw up your life, and that could do it. You have to set your limits, and getting screwed is on the 'will do' side of that equation. The oral thing can be on the 'won't do' side, but always be aware that, when you're overheated, you just might. You have to understand that it's not evil or perverted, it's actually a very natural thing for a lot of people. I don't know how to suggest you ... I haven't the foggiest as to how to overcome the early brainwashing. I don't know if you can.

"John's here. He probably understands that sort of thing a lot better than either of us."

"Put him on," Barney requested. "I've gone this far, talking to you about it, so talking to a real shrink isn't going even that far."

"John Moorehouse here. Mike told me about you, and this is on speaker now. If you want, I'll turn the speaker off."

"No. I don't have any secrets from Mike, already, but only if he's the only other person there."

"I am," Mike replied. "John, would it be a good idea for Barney to meet Larry and Buddy and learn where he really is, or should he run from it, or wait, or what?"

"Very hard call with the information I have, and having never met Barney," John said, seriously. "If you're merely curious, I'd say to forget about it. All you'll do is feed the guilt complex. If you really want to know where you stand in the sexual orientation part, it might be a good idea to resolve what you're feeling now as opposed to what you've been taught you're supposed to feel. I'd say Mike and Eileen are the only two I've ever met who are totally uninhibited, and who carry no guilt of any type. Mike actually can live by the philosophy of, 'Try it. If you don't like it you don't have to do it a second time.'

"I have a few things where I feel guilty for doing something, but I can live with it. I had some religious training when I was a kid, and there's a little of that still hanging around. I know it's a pile of bullshit, intellectually, but it's there.

"You have to make up your mind about it, and you have to be honest with yourself. You mentioned that the oral part was strictly out of the question, but Mike's right. I think I could probably get you hot enough that you would, and know Larry and Buddy could, because what they'd teach you the first round would take it out of the area of logical consideration or anything else. It would be on a reaction basis, and you wouldn't be responsible – but you'd blame yourself after the fact.

"I can also say they wouldn't do that to anyone. The danger you'd put yourself in would be that, due to what they made you feel, you would be damned vulnerable to anyone else who offered that.

"If you can accept that there comes a point where you are in an animal reaction mode, and that you might do things like that, and can cut the guilt complex off with logical internal discourse, I think you'd have a much more open and satisfying life. If you can't, it will destroy you."

There was a long silence, then Barney said, "What's your honest opinion, Mike?"

"That long pause says you should wait, but it also says you will probably be able to handle it when you do decide to try," Mike answered. "Why not wait 'til Saturday to make your decision. Saturday morning. Sleep with a woman Friday night so you'll know if it's curiosity or a need to know. If you decide to go for it, you can spend the whole day, night, and Sunday, and I'll guarantee you that, in that time, you'll do just about everything you swore to yourself you would never do, so go into it with your eyes open wide.

"That will give you time to decide on more than a surface level. I think, *ff* you decide to go for it *honestly*, it won't do you any damage, because you'll have the conflicts decided and at least partially resolved."

"Three days and nights to think it over," Barney agreed. "You can, as you say, consider if it will screw yourself up worse than you are right now."

"You're in a conflicted situation," John said. "Resolve the major parts, then be honest enough with yourself to say it's not wrong or evil, or even negative, because you have to know yourself. Monday, you'll have the tools necessary to know yourself, but you're probably going to lie to yourself about it for awhile.

"Remember the first time you beat off? The instant reaction was chemical, and is almost universal. Did you think, 'I ain't *ever* doing that again!'

"A couple of hours later or next day, you did that again. And again."

Barney laughed. "That is *exactly* what happened, word for word. And it was next day and the next, then twice a day or something, then using things like watermelons. Talk about feeding your guilt! I kept telling myself it was *wrong* and I was going to hell for it – but it felt so *good*!

"Well, if you're going to hell for that, there won't be a single person in heaven!"

"Add it up," Mike said. "Make up your mind to either find out, even if what you find out is that you simply can't do any of it because it's not part of you."

"Okay. I'll do that, and I'll be honest about one more thing," Barney said. "I wanted Ian Forbes to screw me in high school, and made that a reason to stay as far from him as I could, so it couldn't happen.

"You remember him?"

"Sort of a motorcycle bum type? Went for the weight-lifter image? Bad-ass who got knocked over on a drug deal a couple of years ago?" John asked.

"Yup! That was a good one to not experiment with, huh?"

"As you say, 'Yup!'," John agreed.

"I'll be in touch Saturday morning," Barney said. "It'll be yes or no. Not maybe, and not conditional."

<u>*Denouement*</u>

"He'll call right away if he's going for it," John said. "If he's still not sure, it'll be awhile. If he decides not to, it will be a lot later.

"Personally, I think it would be a bad idea. He's just curious and uncertain, and it could mess him up, Mike."

"I know. I'm going to talk him out of it, even if he says he wants to go for it. He doesn't really have the tools, if you know what I mean."

"He's not gay, and he's not going to lose the old ingrained guilt complex," John agreed. "He only thinks he can overcome something like this. He'll actually be relieved if you can talk him out of it. He wants that, deep down. It's something new, and he almost considers it a dare, and he won't back down from a challenge."

They chatted, and Barney called about an hour later. Mike said he was going to the café down the street to use the internet there, because his comp had a virus that was in the process of being cleared out. Barney would meet him there. He grinned at John and headed for the café.

"Greetings, Barney! Come to the wrong conclusion?" Mike greeted.

"Nope! I'm going for it!" Barney replied. "I'll never

know, otherwise."

"You know. You just won't back down from a dare, and it's the wrong decision," Mike said, seriously. "Barney, I like you, and I wouldn't do that to you. I was playing with you. I know damned well that you'd go through with it, and that you'd regret it the rest of your life. You felt an attraction to one guy, and I have some kind of sex magnet about me. You said, yourself, that you couldn't see what the attraction was from a picture. I'm very ordinary, really, but I give off some kind of weird vibration or something that makes people want to go to bed with me.

"John explained how the mixed genetic factor makes almost everyone susceptible to a type of sexual attraction from time to time, but you have to be psychologically equipped to handle it, or it's just plain stupid to play with it.

"What it amounts to is that you'd have the best time in your life with Larry and Buddy, then you'd spend the rest of your life in increasing guilt and doubt about yourself. You're designed by nature to get the greatest pleasure in your life from getting your rocks off, and the fact you liked it so much would just make it worse. You'd start thinking you were actually a screaming fagot who had been lying to yourself all your life, when the exact opposite would be the reality. You're almost totally hetero, but you'd start lying to yourself, thinking you're homo.

"Don't do it. I won't introduce you to my friends, because they'd know it was the wrong thing to do, but they would go for you in a big way, and would probably do everything they could with you.

"You know I'm right. You just feel you were challenged, and you won't back down from a dare."

Barney grinned, and sighed. "Brother! Do you ever have me pegged! I'm more relieved than I can ever remember being before in my life! I was actually shaking on the way here because I don't think I could go through with it. I was scared shitless!"

"You would have gone through with it, and you would have enjoyed the unholy hell out of it, then you would never forgive yourself for giving in to the ultimate evil," Mike said, returning the grin. "I was playing with you, but I think you did learn something. I hope you did."

"I learned that the homophobia bit is about as stupid as it would have been to not back down and admit the romp was the worst thing I could ever do," he agreed. "I think I learned that I won't ever put anyone down again for being queer, because it could happen to me. You showed me that.

"I'll always be curious, though. Maybe that's okay."

"Give me a second?" Mike said. "I have to make a call, then we'll talk a bit more."

He went to the phone and called Norman, who this whole thing started over. He went back to the table to say, "There's a friend coming here to meet you. His name's Norman, and he's gay.

"He wants only straight partners. He doesn't want a man who will do anything more than fuck him and let him blow them. You can learn something about him and yourself without the guilt trip, because you now know that it's a good thing for two people to share something, regardless of what some idiot preacher told you years ago. He'll get exactly what he wants and needs, and you'll get exactly what you want – and need.

"You can turn it down. I really don't know if it will be good for you, in a psychological sense, but I honestly think it will help you grow."

Barney sipped coffee and thought, then nodded. "I think you're probably the best friend I ever had. Nobody ever even spent ten seconds honestly considering whether or not anything was good for me before. It's always been what they want and to hell with how it affects anyone else.

"Know something? I want to hug and kiss you!"

"That would shock hell out of a few here!" Mike said, and they laughed. Eileen came in, and Mike told her that Norman was coming over to lay Barney. Barney looked shocked, then giggled. "I never thought anyone would ever admit to a woman that they were going to get laid by a queer, but it's kind of fun!" he said. "You seem to react ... you didn't react at all!"

"I spent a whole week in bed with John and Mike," she answered. "I doubt there's anything in the world that would surprise me. It's really kind of natural. Why go through some kind of ritual where you act like something is just awful when you know damned well it's the way of the world.

"So! I'll shock you both! I slept with a woman last night! My first time!"

"Like it?" Mike asked.

"No. It probably won't happen again," she replied. "I couldn't wait for it to be over. You can get me off like that in a flash, but she never really got me off at all. I finally faked it so she'd quit. Then she didn't quit. It was almost painful. She was really a nice person, but I wanted her to *go away!*

"Now I envy you because you really get off either and both ways. You stinking lousy arrogant told-you-so bastard asshole son of a bitching motherfucker!"

They laughed and talked about sex until Norman came in. He "visibly brightened" when he saw the date Mike had set him up with, but tried to act like it was just a chance meeting in a café until Eileen took pity on him and said she had to get to work. Barney and Norman left about five minutes later. Mike went home.

"Well?" John greeted.

"Barney's going to lay Norman and Eileen had a lesbian tryst last night," Mike replied.

"Really? She didn't like it, did she?"

"She said it was the longest, most boring night of her life," Mike agreed. "She spent the whole night wanting it to be *over*!"

"Good for her, though," John said, smirking. "She considered it a kind of dare because of us, and she's as bad as that Barney character about never backing down from a dare, no matter how stupid.

"Ed called. He said you have the money, and to come to the office this afternoon to sign the agreement that this is the end of the lawsuit crap."

"I'll be damned glad of that!" Mike said. "So! Now we're millionaires!"

"You are," John replied. "It's your money, Mike. What we have together isn't about money, and must never be. Please."

Mike nodded. "Just so you know, beyond possibility of doubt, that I'll be there for you, anytime, and for any reason, no matter what."

"That, I know," John said. "As much as you know that's a two-way street. All the way and forever." They held each other for a long time.

Later, Mike called Eileen. He said he'd booked a world tour for the three of them that would take a year, then they could decide if they wanted to waste their lives that way or whether they would find something useful to do. They all knew this was a lark, and that they'd go through the money in a year, then be back to "normal" lives.

And that none of them would regret one second of how they'd lived their lives – because their lives would never stop being a learning experience. They were bonded, and would share everything. Eileen would marry and raise a family, as would Mike (probably), but with the understanding that they would never again be apart in any real sense.

There may be a cessation of physical presence, but there would never be a time when they weren't together on another plane. No one ever finds perfection, but it was possible to find something close. You can't decide what's heaven for another, because you'll create hell for them. Trite as it is, no two people are exactly alike. That hasn't and won't happen.

But then, that's what makes life interesting.

C. D. Moulton's works are available on most major outlets as printed or e-books. CD writes the CD Grimes, PI mysteries, the Det. Lt. Nick Storie mysteries, the Clint Faraday mysteries, the Flight of the Maita science fiction series, books on orchid culture and many others of many types. Mystery, adventure, intrigue, science fiction, fantasy, paranormal, mild erotica, and factual.

www.ingramcontent.com/pod-product-compliance
Lightning Source LLC
Chambersburg PA
CBHW051345150726
48000CB00003B/1059